The
Rooster
Who
Refused
To Crow

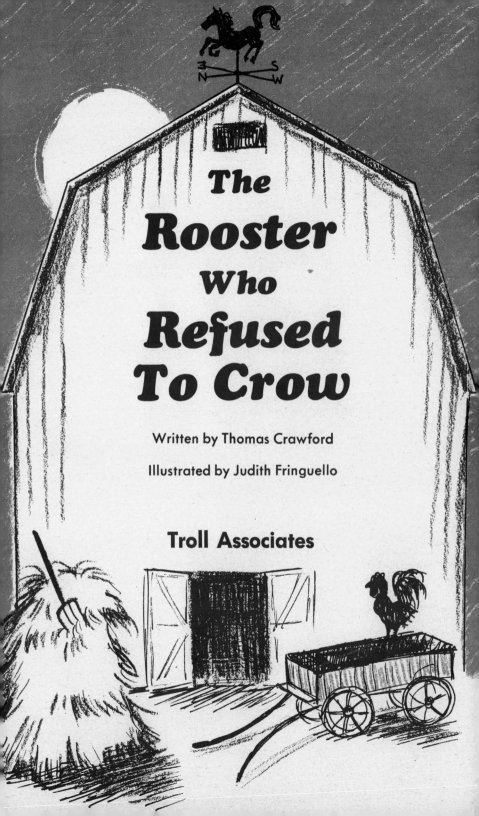

The
Rooster
Who
Refused
To Crow

Written by Thomas Crawford

Illustrated by Judith Fringuello

Troll Associates

The Rooster Who Refused to Crow

"Cock-a-doodle doo! Cock-a-doodle doo!" The sun was just peeping above the horizon. And, as usual, Raffles the rooster was letting everyone know about it.

Every morning it was the same. As soon as the first light of dawn brightened the farmyard, Raffles climbed to the top of the henhouse and crowed as loud as he could.

Of course, he made so much noise, he woke the other animals. Which was just the way it was supposed to be.

Somebody had to wake up the farm. It was a very important job.

If the animals didn't wake up, what would happen?

The cow wouldn't give any milk. The hens wouldn't lay any eggs. And the horse wouldn't pull the wagon.

But most important of all, Farmer Miller wouldn't get up either! And if Farmer Miller didn't get up, the animals wouldn't get any breakfast.

The chickens wouldn't get any grain. The horse wouldn't get any hay. The pigs wouldn't get any corn. And everyone would be hungry and unhappy.

Of course, the animals didn't realize this. They just knew they were sick and tired of listening to that rooster every morning.

"He's always off key," grumbled the cow, who was very proud of her musical moos.

"I dislike the way he struts around the barnyard," complained the pig. "You'd think he brought the sun himself."

"I like to sleep late on Sunday morning," said the horse, "but that rooster and his silly crowing wakes me every time."

And so it went. In the entire farmyard, there wasn't one single animal who was glad the rooster announced the start of day.

Only Farmer Miller was glad, because
he had to get an early start on his chores.
He worked from dawn to dark, plowing,
planting, and taking care of the animals.

But the animals kept grumbling about
Raffles and all the noise he made. They
even called him names behind his back.

OLD LOUDMOUTH   FOGHORN

Then one day, the little rooster learned that the other animals were tired of his crowing.

"That's a fine thing!" he crowed. "I get up early every morning, just to let them know the sun is up, and they don't even appreciate it! Well, just let them try to get up without me. They'll find out!"

With that, the angry rooster stomped off.

The next morning, when the first light of dawn crept into the dark farmyard, the rooster woke up. But he didn't crow. He just sat and waited.

Soon, the bright morning sun was shining down on the farm. But Farmer Miller and the animals in the barn were still fast asleep.

It grew later and later. And still, there was no activity on the farm.

Finally the calves woke up. They started mooing for their breakfasts. But Farmer Miller did not come to feed them.

Then the lambs woke up. They were hungry for their breakfasts. But Farmer Miller did not come to feed them.

Soon, all the animals were making noise. The cow wanted to be milked. The horse wanted to be let out to pasture.

Where
was
Farmer
Miller?

All this while, the rooster watched what was going on. "That'll teach them," he muttered. "That'll show them how much they need me."

At last, when it was almost time for lunch, the farmer came out of the house. He was still rubbing the sleep from his eyes, and in his hurry, he had forgotten to take off his nightcap.

"Dear Me! What has happened?" he wondered. "I didn't hear the rooster this morning. Now I'm behind in all my chores. Dear me, I've got so much work to do, and the day is half over. Dear me."

With that, the farmer ran here and there, trying to do everything at once. Farmer Miller got very mixed up. He hitched the cow up to the wagon...

...and tried to milk the horse...

...and did all sorts of strange things.

"No! No! No!" cried the poor farmer.
"I'm all mixed up. This is all wrong!"
But no matter how hard he tried,
things just got more and more mixed up.

Finally, Farmer Miller gave up. "I'm going back to bed," he said, "and start all over in the morning."

That night, all the animals had a meeting in the barn. All except the rooster. He just stayed in the henhouse and chuckled over what had happened.

The horse spoke first. "Something must be done," he said. "Everyone over-slept this morning, and things were all mixed up. Something must be done."

"Yes!" exclaimed the other animals. "This simply won't do. Someone has to wake us up in the morning."

"And Farmer Miller, too," said the cow. "But we can't ask the rooster — not after the way we complained about his crowing."

"I have an idea," said the pig. "Let's take turns announcing the start of day. I will do it tomorrow morning. The goat can do it the next day, and so on. That way, we won't need the rooster."

"That's a wonderful idea," cried the animals. Everyone agreed that taking turns was the best way to solve the problem.

Next morning, just as the sun came up, the pig woke up.

Immediately, he went to the door of his pen and oinked as loud as he could.

But his loudest oink was not nearly loud enough. Not one animal heard him. And especially not Farmer Miller, who was fast asleep in the house.

When the farmer finally did get up, it was even later than the day before. And he made an even worse mess of things.

The next morning it was the goat's turn.

As soon as the sun came up, he tried to wake the others. He tried as hard as he could, but it was no use. He wasn't loud enough either, and Farmer Miller did not come out until late afternoon.

The next morning it was the horse's turn. The night before, he told the other animals he would make so much noise, Farmer Miller would be sure to wake up.

But a strange thing happened. The
horse slept right through the sunrise.
In fact, the cow had to come over and
kick on his door to wake him up.

Well, this went on for almost a week, and not one morning did it work. In fact, the last day, Farmer Miller did not come out at all. He spent the entire day sleeping peacefully in his bed.

Something had to be done fast, before the farm was ruined!

The animals held another meeting in the barn. There was a lot of arguing and each blamed the other for not waking the farmer.

But deep down inside, they all knew what was wrong: It was the rooster's job to wake up the farm. He was the only one who could do it right.

At last, the cow, who was older and somewhat wiser than the rest, suggested a solution. "I think we should all go to the rooster and apologize," she said.

"We've been very unkind to him. After all, he was only trying to do his job. If we tell him we're sorry, maybe he'll agree to announce the day again."

After listening to the cow, they all decided it was a good idea to ask the rooster's pardon.

One by one, the animals told the rooster they were sorry.

Sure enough, as soon as the animals had apologized, the rooster was more than happy to go back to his old job.

And the very next morning, at the first light of day, the happy rooster was crowing as loud as he could.

"Cock-a-doodle doo!" he crowed. "Cock-a-doodle doo!"

And even before the rooster stopped crowing, Farmer Miller rushed out of his house to start his chores.

And he didn't mix anything up either. He did everything just right.

What a wonderful day!